Book I

MY FUN-TO-READ BOOKS

Stories for enjoyment and enrichment

Text adapted by James Ertel

THE SOUTHWESTERN COMPANY • Nashville

JOEY'S HORSE

Illustrations by Dan Siculan

THE SOUTHWESTERN COMPANY • Nashville

The true-to-life photographs in this book were taken especially for the Southwestern Company by Bill McNabb, Jr. at Meadow Creek Ranch, Auburn, California.

The photo on page three was taken by Charles Reynolds at Oak Brook, Illinois.

The design of the book is by Alex D'Amato. Supervision of color reproduction is by Don Walkoe.

Joey lived on a horse farm.
    Joey's day always began with
a visit to the stables.
    Each horse in the stable lived
in its own stall.

Joey's favorite horse was named Lady Jane. She was always quiet and gentle with him.

Joey always made sure that Lady Jane had fresh hay and oats.

He brushed her coat until it was smooth and shiny.

On sunny days Joey would
ride Lady Jane. He liked to ride
her through the green woods.

When they got back, Joey
would rub Lady Jane with a
towel so she would not catch cold.
Then he would give her a
special treat—a carrot.

Joey watched the blacksmith
put new shoes on Lady Jane.
Lady Jane wore iron shoes.

One day Joey saw his father and a stranger looking at Lady Jane.

The man and Joey's father went to the stable door. The stranger looked at Lady Jane's teeth in the bright sunlight.

Joey knew his father made money selling horses.

The man felt Lady Jane's feet.
He asked Joey's father, "How
much do you want for this horse?"
Joey did not wait to hear his
father's answer.
Joey ran to his room.

From his window, Joey could
see the man pulling Lady Jane to
a truck.

Joey's father was helping the
man get Lady Jane on the truck.

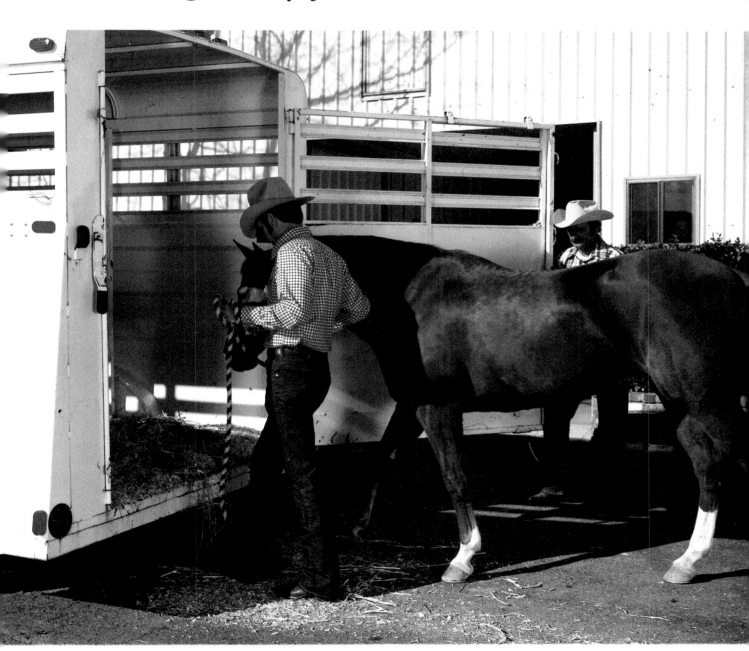

Joey ran outside. The truck
was driving away.
   Joey's father was waving.
"Lady Jane will have a nice
home," he said to Joey.

Joey went to Lady Jane's empty
stall. He kicked the fresh hay he had
brought in for her.

Then Joey went out and lay down
under a big tree.

Lady Jane was not happy in her new home.

She was put in a field with other horses, but she stayed off by herself.

The new owner liked horses.
He tried to be kind to Lady
Jane. But Lady Jane would not let
him ride her.
Every time he tried to lead
Lady Jane to her new stall she
pulled against the rope.

The new owner scratched his head. He had never seen a horse act this way.

He decided to get rid of her.

He sold Lady Jane to another man. This man led Lady Jane away to his stable.

The next owner was not kind.

"I understand you cause trouble,"
he said to Lady Jane.

He hit Lady Jane across the nose
with a rope.

He slammed the door of her
stall and went away.

After the man was gone,
Lady Jane kicked the door.

It opened. The man had not locked it.

Lady Jane walked out into the farm yard.

She came to a fence and a gate. She pushed at the gate many, many times with her nose.

Finally it opened.
She was free!

Lady Jane ran across a field.

She did not know where she was going. She was looking for home.

She found a road and followed it.

She got hungry and stopped to eat grass. Cows were in the same field.

Night came.

Lady Jane walked on and on. She had no idea where she was or where she was going.

She was tired. Her feet hurt. But she kept walking.

She walked along many roads.
None of them were ones she knew.
In the middle of the night
Lady Jane came to a road she knew
before. The road led to another.
That road led to Joey's house.

After a long time the sun
came up.

Lady Jane stood by the back
door. She just waited.

The sun shone into Joey's window.

He woke up.

He got dressed slowly. He
still missed Lady Jane.

Joey's mother called, "Joey, time for breakfast."

"I'm coming," said Joey sleepily.

He ate breakfast. Then he said, "I'm going outside."

He opened the back door and there stood Lady Jane. Joey could not believe it.

He ran to Lady Jane and hugged her.

Joey led Lady Jane to her old stall.

He brushed her and gave her fresh hay.

Then he ran to the house.

"Dad," he called, "Lady Jane is back."

"Dad, please can we keep her?" asked Joey.

"Joey, I don't know," said his father.

"Please, dad, this is her home," said Joey.

"I will see what we can do," said his father.

That night Joey could not sleep.

He waited till the moon came up
and his parents were asleep.

Then he took a blanket and
went to the stables.

He lay down on the hay in
Lady Jane's stall and fell asleep.

Lady Jane watched over him
through the night.

Early the next morning Joey rode
Lady Jane through the woods.

When they got back, Joey's father
said to him, "I have good news.
I bought Lady Jane back."

Joey looked at his father.

"She's your horse," he said.

Katie's
ZOO

Drawings by David Cunningham

THE SOUTHWESTERN COMPANY • Nashville

The majority of true-to-life photographs in this book were taken especially for Encyclopaedia Britannica Press by Lyle Mayer at Brookfield Zoo, Brookfield, Illinois. The Press is deeply grateful to Mr. Robert Bean, Director, for permission to photograph the animals, and to his staff for their cooperation.

Other photographs were taken by the following photographers in various locations: Charles Reynolds, lion and gorilla; Dr. Wendel Swanson, polar bear; William Deneen, koala; Lynwood Chace, toucan; and Weldon Johnson, flamingos.

The design of the book is by Ruth Rooney. Supervision of color reproduction is by James Lockhart.

Katie can look out her window
and see baboons and African sheep.
Katie's father is a zookeeper.
She lives in a house in a zoo.

Each day Katie watches the baboons and sheep. They get along fine together.

In winter the baboons are taken to the Monkey House. The sheep stay out all winter.

Katie is friendly to all the animals in the zoo.

One of her favorites is a young animal called a llama.

Katie named this llama Snowball. He was born in South America.

Katie likes to feel the large,
white tusks on Zuma, a three-year-
old elephant from India.

Ted, a zoo keeper, cares for
Zuma.

Some days after school,
Katie takes Reggie the reindeer
for a stroll.

Reindeers live in the far
north, where it is very cold.

Katie loves to cuddle Penny, the white and black French lop-eared rabbit.

How are Penny's ears different from other rabbits you have seen?

Some of the orangutans in Katie's zoo love to climb down a wooden ladder into their large pen.

Orangutans live in trees and most come from Borneo in Asia.

Katie likes to help fix
breakfast for the animals.
　　Most of the animals eat
vegetables for breakfast.
　　Katie cuts fresh carrots
for the animals.

Frank and Fritz, two of the
pigs in the zoo, get a snack from
their friend Katie.
Frank, the black pig, is
about four months old. Fritz, the
lighter colored pig, is an adult.

Katie feeds Jeff, a young
angora goat, a bottle of milk.
Angora sweaters are made from
the wool of goats like Jeff.

Katie watches Otto feed bread
to Harry, a pygmy hippo.

A pygmy hippo is a very small
hippo with short legs.

There are only a few pygmy
hippos left in the world.

Katie sees Andrew waking up.

Andrew is the biggest lion in the Lion House.

Andrew is not mean, but Katie knows she should not pet him.

Mabel, the tiger, looks at Katie when Katie stops at the cage.

Mabel's three children look at Katie, too.

Katie waves to them.

Katie's father is holding a
baby gorilla from Africa.
    Daddy will ask Katie to
pick a name for this playful new
zoo animal.

One of Katie's favorite animal friends is Freddie the ferret. When Katie is not playing with him, Freddie likes to dig holes in the ground.

Freddie's paws are very good for digging.

There is a hospital building
in Katie's zoo.

A monkey named Bing has been
sneezing with a cold.

He is in an incubator. The
incubator keeps him warm and helps
him get well faster.

Dr. Ray is the zoo doctor.
He has to know how to take care
of all kinds of sick animals.

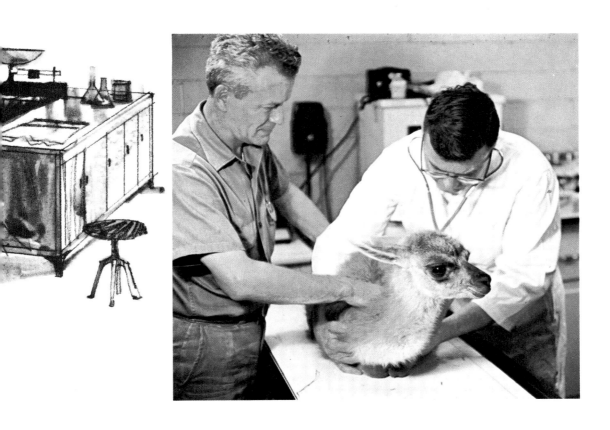

His hospital is almost the same
as a hospital for people.

Katie's zoo has animals that
come out only at night.
Some of these are kinkajous,
from South America.
Kinkajous like to eat bananas.

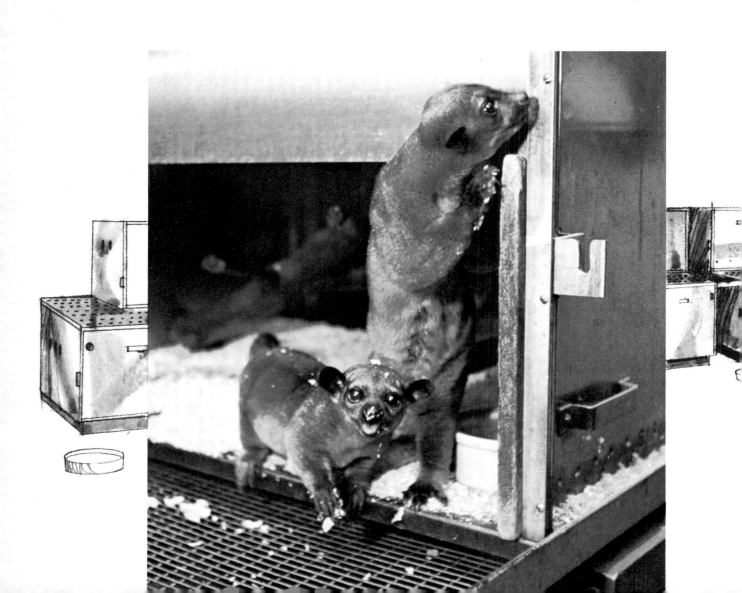

Another night animal in Katie's zoo is called a cuscus.

He has big eyes and a long tail.

A cuscus sleeps like a tiny ball on a branch in a tree.

Katie's zoo has bears.
There are white polar bears.
They like to splash in their pool.
There are giant Kodiak bears
from Alaska. They are bigger
than a large man.

This large animal is Ray the rhinoceros.

He has very thick skin and two horns on his snout. Rhinos come from Africa and Asia.

Even the baby giraffe makes
Katie feel small.

The baby was born only two
days ago, but already he is much
taller than Katie.

Katie watches Kim swing
from branch to branch.
He is a koala from Australia.
"He looks like a teddy bear,"
says Katie.

Betty the boa is just one of
many snakes at Katie's zoo. Betty
came to the zoo from Mexico.
Many people think these snakes
are poisonous, but they are not.

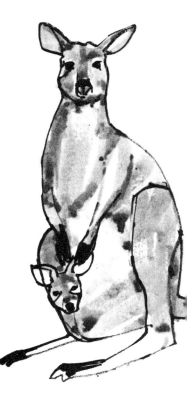

There are birds in Katie's zoo.
One of the strangest of them is
called a toucan.

The toucan has a beak almost
as big as his body.

The flamingos have very thin legs and long necks. Katie likes their pretty pink color.

There are also penguins in the zoo. They live in a special pool with icy water.

The Dolphin House is one of Katie's favorite places in the zoo. Each day the dolphins greet her. She likes to watch Al, their trainer, teach the dolphins to do their tricks.

A special friend of Katie is Yakie the Yak. Yakie was born at Katie's zoo, but his family was born in Asia.

Sometimes Yakie gets lonely, but Katie keeps him company.

"Don't worry, Yakie," says Katie. "You'll like it here in the zoo."

Jamie's Dog

Illustrations by Don Rodell

THE SOUTHWESTERN COMPANY • Nashville

The true-to-life photographs in this book are from the educational motion picture "Roy, Sheep Dog of the Scottish Highlands," produced for Encyclopaedia Britannica Films, Inc., by John Barnes, directed by Garry Levy, and photographed at Moniaive, Dumfriesshire, Scotland, by Bryan Everett.

The design of this book is by Alex D'Amato. Supervision of color reproduction is by James Lockhart.

Jamie and his dog, Roy live on
a farm in Scotland.

The farmers here raise sheep.

The sheep are looked after by
well trained dogs.

The work of a sheep dog is
not easy. He must move them to
new fields for fresh grass. He has
to make sure no sheep gets lost.

One afternoon Jamie and his
father were out on the hills with
Roy. Roy was learning his work.
    Jamie's father was trying to
teach Roy whistle signals.
    Roy kept making mistakes.
Jamie looked worried.

At last Roy got the sheep into
the pen for the night.

'He's not a good dog, Jamie,"
he said. "Roy doesn't obey
the whistle quickly enough."

"Let's go home," Father said. He whistled for Roy.

Just then Roy saw a rabbit. He ran after it.

"After a rabbit! That's the worst thing a sheep dog could do," Father scolded. "We'll have to get another dog."

"Roy's just learning, Father. Give him a chance," said Jamie.

"No, no," Father said. "Roy's too frisky. He'll never make a good sheep dog."

When they got near the house,
there was no sign of Roy.
Sheep were standing around.
Father shook his head.

"What happened to Roy?" asked Jamie's mother.

"Gone after a rabbit," said Father. "He's no good."

After dinner Jamie sat by the fire. He listened for Roy's bark.

Jamie's mother stopped sewing. "Don't worry, Jamie," she said. "Roy will come home. When he gets hungry, he'll be home."

Jamie read a magazine.

"Look!" he said to his mother. "The sheep dog contest. It will be in October."

"Roy's young and has a lot to learn yet, Jamie," said his mother.

"He could learn this summer, Mother," Jamie answered. "I know he's a smart dog."

His father looked up from his
magazine.

"And what if he saw a rabbit at
the contest?" said his father.
He'd forget again. No, I'm sorry.
We must look for another dog."

Father's voice was stern.

Jamie went to his room. For a long time he looked out the window.

The moon came up and still Jamie looked at the hills. No Roy.

"Oh, Roy," Jamie whispered. "I know you're not a bad dog. Maybe you're hurt."

He went to bed. For a long time he was awake, listening.

Early the next morning, Jamie
heard loud barking. He ran to the
window. There was Roy!

Jamie dressed and ran outside.
"What is it, boy?" he said.

Roy jumped up at him, barking.
Then he ran to the farm gate.

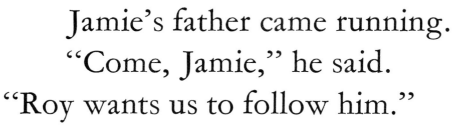

Jamie's father came running.
"Come, Jamie," he said.
"Roy wants us to follow him."
Roy raced ahead up the hill.
Jamie and his father followed.

When they got to the top of
the hill, they could not see Roy.
Father whistled.

They heard a bark. Father
and Jamie followed the sound.

Roy was standing by a sheep that had gotten lost.

Roy had found the sheep and had stayed with it all night.

"Well, Jamie," Father said, "that was a fine thing Roy did."

Roy worked hard all that day.

That night, Jamie lay down beside Roy. He read in the magazine about the sheep dog contest. Father looked at him.

"Well, Jamie," he said, "Maybe we'll keep Roy after all."

"He'll go on to the contest, too, won't he, Father?" said Jamie.

"We'll see about that," Father said. "He must work hard."

Every day that summer Roy
was on the hills with the sheep.
Roy learned quickly and well.
He sometimes made mistakes, but
Father was patient with him. Roy
learned to understand the whistle
signals, and how to control the
herd of sheep.

Jamie watched Roy work. To get the sheep moving, Roy ran back and forth, barking.

He learned how to make them go to the right or left.

He did not hurt or frighten the sheep. If they feared him, they would run away from him.

By late summer Roy could manage the sheep well. He understood every whistle. Father trusted him with the sheep.

One evening, Father said to Jamie, "Well, do you still think he'll make a champion?"

"I certainly do," Jamie said.

Autumn came. The leaves
changed color to red and orange.

As the day of the sheep dog
contest came near, there was much
talk about it.

"Roy's good," Father said.
"But the best dogs in the country
will be there. Only one can
be the champion."

The day of the contest came. Jamie and his parents went to the contest grounds.

"Are you nervous, Jamie?" Father asked him.

"A little bit," Jamie said.

Jamie looked out at the field
where the contest had just started.
On the field, the first dog
was working.
He was obeying whistle signals
from his master.

Each dog had two tests.
First, it had to make the sheep
go between two flags. Then it
had to make them go into a pen.

The dogs were all good
and it was hard to tell which
was best.

"That one will be hard to
beat," said Father as one dog
left the field.

Roy was the last dog.

Father whistled, and Roy ran.
In the first test he had to
drive the sheep between two
gates. Time was important.
He tried to drive the sheep
forward. They would not move.

Finally the sheep ran. Roy
steered them toward the gates.
The judges watched closely.
"Come on, boy," Jamie
whispered. Roy was working
alone. At last the sheep were
through. It was a good run.

In the second test, Roy had
to get the sheep into a pen.
Now Father went out on the
field to work with Roy.

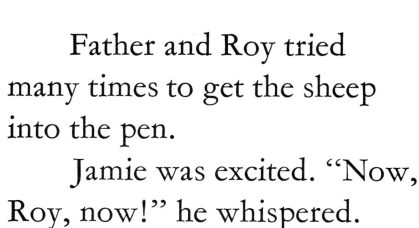

Father and Roy tried
many times to get the sheep
into the pen.

Jamie was excited. "Now,
Roy, now!" he whispered.
One sheep tried to run away.
Roy chased it back.

The people were very quiet.
"Good dog," one man said.
The sheep were nervous.
Father whistled and Roy barked.
Suddenly the sheep ran into
the pen. Father shut the gate.

"Good job, Roy!" called
Jamie.

Jamie and his parents waited
to hear the names of the winners.

"First, Mr. Stewart's Bob,"
called the announcer.

"Second, Mr. Cameron's Nell."
Then the third name was called.

It was Roy!

Jamie went with his
father and Roy to get
the silver cup.

The next day Roy was out on the hills again with Father and Jamie.

Roy had won third prize, but he was not yet a champion.

Jamie was glad that he had believed in Roy all the time.

"You were right about Roy, Jamie," his father said as they walked home. "He's a good dog."

"He is," said Jamie, "and one day he'll be the champion of Scotland. I know he will."